This book is dedicated to all the amazing warriors
Who have fought battles among themselves, lost
their love and friendship but still have managed
to survive.

THE AMBIGUITY IN ME

Ghizlan Javaid

Illustrations by Isha Barlas

Forever indebted to my dad Javaid Feroze who had been my strength throughout my life without a doubt.

Abu, I pray that you are always smiling up in the Heaven. Also, a massive thank you to my mum Lubna, without her support this book would not have been possible. Most importantly a thank you to my husband and children who do not seize to inspire me daily.

Table Of Contents

Preface

These short collections of fictional poems
initiate from falling in love followed by
being broken hearted, finally accepting
the reality and moving on with life. This all
may seem ambiguous to some readers but
all, sometimes life does not give us any choice
other than that.
Life is precious and beautiful. Though a
dream broken can be hard to handle but
life should not stop there. It should be
celebrated every day. Acceptance of current
situations and surroundings provide peace of
heart and contentment.

Happy reading!

You And I

Just You And I
hand in hand by the sea,
waves dwelling onto our feet.
Dark starry night,
yet so bright.
Us making memories along this ride
cherishing the time,
when we are in each other's sight.
And never to deprive,
one another,
from the love that thrives.
Promises being made
to not to go astray.
Keeping faith and never betray.
Just you and I
hand in hand by the sea.

Pixie Dust

Our love is
like a pixie dust
It sparkles
and glows
Yet it remains untold.
Of all the glory
that it does hold,
shine brighter than the
whole world alone.
As you and I
 created our own universe,
just you, me and nothing
between us!

Discreet Love

Let us fall once again in love,
back track to the time
when the days were long
and the nights were so young.
Let us fall once again in love,
visualise our long walks
along the bunches of roses
with no thorns.
Our never-ending discussions
that would lead to meaningful conversations.
Let us fall once again in love,
this time, keeping it all discreet.
So, it does not get rough!

Tranquillity

Probably it was another summer fling?
that unknowingly made us to cling.
The feelings we shared
were more than we cared?
of the opinion
that everyone dared.
I wish you had not been so impatient,
a bit hasty in making decisions.
Rather I wanted you to stay put
keeping faith,
and not losing hope
But you paid no heed.
Walked onto a path
that led us to depart
and left me broken heart.
It brutally took away my tranquillity,
yet again abandoning me,
with my ambiguity.

Endless Wait

You went and took my
soul with you,
The hurt that felt,
and the numbness caused
shall never pause.
Now I just wander
aimlessly
waiting to meet
my ambiguity
yet again.

Memory Of You

You left and
my life hit a pause.
My heart was stuck
in a loop,
that revolved
around the past.
I thought
I missed you,
found it hard to steer
thoughts without you.
But actually, I was not
in love with you.
Maybe a little in love
with the
memory of you.

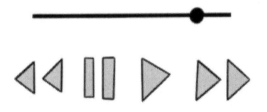

Two Rivers

You asked me to leave,
compelled me to go away,
that led me to foresee.
The future that
could not ever be.
Leaving me behind
and yourself moving forward
eventually made me realise
that decision was very wise.
As we are like two rivers
That do flow together
But are never ready to mingle.

Promises

I know you are hurting,
the pain that
you are enduring.
But you have a unique
way of showing.
Pushing me away.
Shutting me down.
Will all the sorrows be gone?
I know you have
promises to keep,
that are vital to you
and hold meanings too deep.
Let me be around,
so I can shun the sorrows
that surround.
Let me stay and do not push away,
as without you my heart would astray.

Good In A Goodbye

I have heard people say,
there is good in goodbyes.
But if it is true
then why does it hurt,
when I am not with you.
I know this too shall pass
but will it last?
I am drench in sorrow,
anticipating for a better tomorrow.
If still you decide,
not to unite,
I would like to make it right.
 You did not conform to me in this life,
I elect to remain a stranger
in the afterlife!

A Wish

I sit here all day long,
and that too all alone.
Rejoicing in the hollow,
pleasure of my solitude.
Savouring the taste of,
its sweet emptiness.
I look around,
and you are nowhere
to be found.
I wait for a while,
then in my mind,
I eventually realise,
that you were nothing
but a wish.
A mere mist.
That in a glimpse
just vanished.

Chasing Shadows

I stand here all alone,
with darkness that surrounds,
And you are nowhere to be found.
I try to turn around,
in a hope to look again,
I see a face,
so kind and sane.
I walk towards the shadow.
Leaving behind the sorrow.
I take your hand,
you turn around
And take me beyond
the clear clouds.
Away from the darkness,
revealing only freshness.
Now that you are here,
there are no more tears.
And all my fears
have disappeared.
I want you to stay
And never go away.
So the darkness that prevailed,
shall never be there again!

Hollow Dream

I climbed onto the stairs
of the clouds,
just to follow a dream.
Do not know what for.
But now halfway through,
I realise that I can never reach,
what I believed was true.
I ask myself,
Why did I leave the world of reality?
just to follow a fantasy.
I defied all the odds,
just to hold onto a dream.
Now when I look back and try to find,
what I had left behind,
I see nothing but a mist of my dreams.
Blinding me from all that was real.
No one can imagine the way I feel.
A web of silence,
A whole network of violence,
That too in my mind.
Tell me, is it so bad,
to follow a dream.

Fiction

Walking down the
memory lane,
I just cannot get
past that heartache.
Your beautiful laughter,
echoes in my ears.
Your dreamy eyes,
were enough to mesmerise.
The affection that
you had shown,
When I was in my lows,
cohered till now to my existence.
Even though I admit
that there
was some resistance.
Is it just me,
Or you too had addiction,
to the long gone past fiction?

Ambiguity Prevails

The echoes of the muted shore,
the silence of the grainy sand
jolted my thoughts,
to make me comprehend.
That there is always some calm
before the storm.
It brought back the thunder
of my memories,
reminiscing those times.
just us being together
 and no one to bother.
But that changed quickly
only leaving me behind
with my ambiguity.

Lost Cause

I was holding on to a thought
just a lost cause,
that was long gone,
I was adamant to the fact,
and made believe myself,
that my life revolved around that shell.
It had to be broken,
reality needed to snap open.
For those pieces to be shattered
across my soul.
Only to make myself understand
that it was nothing,
but just a mere case of distress.

Cutting Ties

We went our separate ways,
parted our paths,
and promised
never to come across.
It took me a while,
which seemed like
an entire life,
to accept that element.
But I never had thought
that cutting all ties,
would make me realise,
what a blessing
it was in a disguise.

I Shall Rise

I see a bright light
down the winding lane
I walk towards the end
But I find myself in sheer distress.
The light that I saw
was nothing but false.
It was the shadow of my dreams,
that I had once in my mind.
I was left all shaken,
when they got broken.
Taking away my smile
and making me wonder
would I ever again rise?
But I walk through the light
leaving the distress behind.
With a hope in my mind,
that the sun would again shine
making my world so bright.
As I still do believe
that after the rain goes
there are rainbows!

Freedom

Today my heart
sets you free,
In order to breathe.
I hope you can now see
The hurt in me.
The truth is
that we were
never meant to be.
Only return if
you promise to be,
forever my companion
with my ambiguity.

AUTHOR'S NOTE

Sometimes life puts you in a situation
where you are bound to make a choice.
 Always choose wisely. Love always
wins but not necessarily you end up
getting what your heart desires. You
might not feel at that point, but the
future might be brighter than your
current situation that you are in.
Give yourself some breathing space.
Evaluate your thoughts and let some
 ambiguity linger on.

Love Always,

Ghiz

Printed in Great Britain
by Amazon